This Little Tiger book belongs to:

_____

_____

_____

For my mother, who taught me to see what is beautiful,
and my father, who showed me the joy of giving
~ GL

for Kirsty, with love
~ GH

LITTLE TIGER PRESS LTD,
an imprint of the Little Tiger Group
I The Coda Centre, 189 Munster Road, London SW6 6AW
www.littletiger.co.uk

First published in Great Britain 2003
This edition published 2016
Text copyright © Gillian Lobel 2003
Illustrations copyright © Gaby Hansen 2003
Gillian Lobel and Gaby Hansen have asserted their rights
to be identified as the author and illustrator of this work
under the Copyright, Designs and Patents Act, 1988

ISBN 978-1-84869-463-7
Printed in China • LTP/1800/1901/0417

1 3 5 7 9 10 8 6 4 2

LITTLE BEAR'S
SPECIAL
WISH

GILLIAN LOBEL

GABY HANSEN

LITTLE TIGER PRESS
London

The sun was still in bed when
Little Brown Bear crept out into
the shadowy woods.

"I wish, I wish . . ." he whispered.

"You're up early, Little Brown Bear!" called
Lippity Rabbit. "What are you wishing for?"

"It's my mummy's birthday," said Little
Brown Bear, "and I wish I could find the most
special present in all the world for her."

"I'll help you!" said Lippity Rabbit.
So off they went along the winding path. Little
pools of moonlight danced around their feet.

In the middle of the woods was a big rock.

Little Brown Bear sat down for a moment to think. High above him glittered a star, so big and bright he could almost touch it.

"I know – I could give my mummy a star," he said. "That would be a very special present."

Little Brown Bear gave
a little jump. But he could
not reach the star.

He gave a very big jump.
But still he could not reach
the star. Then Little Brown
Bear had an idea.

"I know!" he said. "If we climb to the very top of the hill, then we will be able to reach the stars!"

From the top of the hill the stars looked even brighter – and much nearer, too. Little Brown Bear stretched up on to his tiptoes. But the stars were still too far away. Then Little Brown Bear had a very good idea indeed.

"I know!" he said. "We must build
a big, big tower to the stars!"
    "I'll help you!" said
Lippity Rabbit.

Together they piled the biggest stones they could find,
one on top of the other. Then they stepped back and looked.
A stone stairway stretched to the stars.
    "Now I shall reach a star for my mummy," said Little
Brown Bear happily. He climbed right to the top and
stretched out a paw. But still he couldn't reach the stars.

"I know!" called Lippity Rabbit. "If I climb on your shoulders, then I can knock a star down with my long, loppy ears!"

Lippity Rabbit scrambled on to Little Brown Bear's shoulders. He stretched up his long, loppy ears. He waggled them furiously.

"Be careful, Lippity!" called Little Brown Bear. "You're making me wobble!"

Suddenly Little Brown Bear felt something tapping his foot.

"Can I help you?" croaked a voice.

"Why yes, Very Small Frog," said Little Brown Bear. "Are you any good at jumping?"

Very Small Frog puffed out his chest. "Just watch me!" he said. High into the air he flew, and landed right between Lippity Rabbit's long, loppy ears.

"Can you reach the brightest star from there?" asked Little Brown Bear.

"No problem!" shouted Very Small Frog.

He took a mighty breath. "Look out, stars, here I come!" he shouted.

Very Small Frog gave a great push with his strong back legs. Up, up, up he sailed. Lippity Rabbit's long, loppy ears twirled round and round.

"Help!" he shouted. "Somebody save me!"

Backwards and forwards he swayed, and backwards and forwards swayed Little Brown Bear. With a mighty crash the stone tower toppled to the ground. And down and down tumbled Lippity Rabbit and Little Brown Bear.

"I can't breathe, Lippity!" gasped Little Brown Bear. "You're sitting right on by dose!"

Then Very Small Frog sailed down from the stars and landed on Lippity Rabbit's head.

"I'm sorry, Little Brown Bear," he said. "I jumped right over the moon, but I still couldn't reach the stars."

Little Brown Bear sat up carefully. His nose was scratched and his head hurt.

"Now my special wish will *never* come true," he said. "I shall never find a star for my mummy!"

"Don't be sad, Little Brown Bear," said Lippity Rabbit. And he gave him a big hug.

A tear ran down Little Brown Bear's nose, and splashed into a tiny pool at his feet.

As he rubbed his eyes, Little Brown Bear saw something that danced and sparkled in the shining water. Surely it was his star! Little Brown Bear jumped up with excitement.

"Now I know what to do!" he cried.

Off he ran down the hillside.
"Wait for us!" cried Lippity Rabbit
and Very Small Frog.

Through the ferny woods they ran, over the silver meadows, until they reached the stream. For a long time they hunted along the sandy shore until Little Brown Bear found just what he was looking for. Then carefully, carefully, he carried it all the way home.

"Happy birthday, Mummy!" he cried.

Into his mother's lap he placed a pearly shell that shone like a rainbow. There, in the heart of the shell, a tiny pool of water quivered. And in that pool a very special star shimmered and shook – the star that had made a little bear's birthday wish come true.

"Lippity Rabbit and Very Small Frog helped me find the shell, but I caught the star all by myself!" said Little Brown Bear proudly.

Mother Bear knelt down and gave him a big hug.

"Thank you all very much," she said. "This is a very special birthday present indeed!"